Robert Muchamore was born in 1972 and spent thirteen years working as a private investigator.

The CHERUB series has won numerous awards, including the 2005 Red House Children's Book Award. For more information on Robert and his work, visit **www.cherubcampus.com**.

Praise for the CHERUB series:
'If you can't bear to read another story about elves, princesses or spoiled rich kids who never go to the toilet, try this. You won't regret it.' *The Ultimate Teen Book Guide*

'My sixteen-year-old son read *The Recruit* in one sitting, then went out the next day and got the sequel.' Sophie Smiley, teacher and children's author

'So good I forced my friends to read it, and they're glad I did!' Helen, age 14

'CHERUB is the first book I ever read cover to cover. It was amazing.' Scott, age 13

'The best book ever.' Madeline, age 12

'CHERUB is a must for Alex Rider lovers.' Travis, age 14

The CHERUB series by Robert Muchamore:

DARK SUN
Robert Muchamore

Hodder
Children's
Books

A division of Hachette Children's Books

A Catalogue record for this book is available ·
from the British Library

ISBN-13: 978 0 340 95679 3 (home)
ISBN-13: 978 0 340 95680 9 (export)

Typeset in Goudy by Avon DataSet Ltd,
Bidford-on-Avon, Warwickshire

Printed and bound in Great Britain by
CPI Bookmarque, Croydon, CR0 4TD

Cover repro by Saxon Photolitho, Norwich, Norfolk

The text paper within this book was donated by Abitibi
Consolidated and Paper Management Services Ltd

The paper and board used in this paperback by
Hodder Children's Books are natural recyclable products
made from wood grown in sustainable forests.
The manufacturing processes conform to the
environmental regulations of the country of origin.

Hodder Children's Books
a division of Hachette Children's Books
338 Euston Road, London NW1 3BH
An Hachette Livre UK company

WHAT IS CHERUB?

CHERUB is a branch of British Intelligence. Its agents are aged between ten and seventeen years. Cherubs are mainly orphans who have been taken out of care homes and trained to work undercover. They live on CHERUB campus, a secret facility hidden in the English countryside.

WHAT USE ARE KIDS?

Quite a lot. Nobody realises kids do undercover missions, which means they can get away with all kinds of stuff that adults can't.

WHO ARE THEY?

About three hundred children live on CHERUB campus. Among the agents are fifteen-year-old JAMES ADAMS and his twelve-year-old sister LAUREN. Their friends include BRUCE NORRIS, ANDY LAGAN and Lauren's on-off boyfriend 'RAT' RATHBONE.

CHERUB T-SHIRTS

Cherubs are ranked according to the colour of the T-shirts they wear on campus. ORANGE is for visitors. RED is for kids who live on CHERUB campus but are too young to qualify as agents (the minimum age is ten). BLUE is for kids undergoing CHERUB's tough one-hundred-day basic training regime. A GREY T-shirt means you're qualified for missions. NAVY is a reward for outstanding performance on a single mission. The BLACK T-shirt is the ultimate recognition for outstanding achievement over a number of missions.

1. RANCID

July 2007

Honeywill Community School was a dump, but it was the last day before summer holidays so at least everyone was happy. Teachers who hadn't cracked a smile since September let classes play Nintendo in the sun, the headmaster was bounding around in sunglasses and tennis shorts. Kids even took beatings with good grace, knowing their next appointment with the bullies wouldn't be for at least six weeks.

All the displays had been torn off the walls in Greg's second-floor form room. He stood on a chair, leaning out of the classroom window with his school tie fixed around his head like a bandana and all his shirt buttons undone. Lunchtime was in full flow on the concrete playground below: girls chatting in huddles, boys playing football and a massive queue at the water fountain because it was the hottest day of the year so far.

'Smell that,' Zhang said, as the overweight Chinese boy thrust a clear plastic tub up towards Greg's nostrils.

The stench hit Greg like a fist. He recoiled violently, jumping off the chair and almost sprawling out as he backed into a metal paper basket.

'You *know* it's bad!' Zhang grinned, swinging the pot back towards Greg's nose.

'Get off!' Greg shouted, coughing and retching as he scrambled away between desks. 'Is that your mum's cooking?'

Zhang shook his head as he placed the lid back on the tub. 'It's coleslaw from the school canteen. Says use by November fourteenth, but I just found it at the back of my locker.'

The third boy in the classroom was a skinny lad called George and he was cracking up laughing.

'Shut your mouth, stick boy,' Greg shouted. 'Unless you want me to rub your face in it.'

But now that the lid was safely back on the coleslaw, Greg saw the funny side himself and he smiled even more when he saw the mound of junk Zhang had cleared out of his locker: text books covered in mud where Zhang had dumped his football boots on top of them, food wrappers, dirty tissues and a bottle of correction fluid that had leaked over his exercise books and dried into a hard white lump.

'Animal,' Greg snorted. 'Is that a locker or a TARDIS? I don't even know how all that junk fitted in there.'

Zhang's bulky frame swaggered across the room towards his two mates. 'Greg, your locker's neat because you've only been at this school for half a term.'

George shook his head. 'No Zhang, his locker's neat because he's not a revolting fat slob.'

Zhang didn't like being called fat and stepped up to George to face him off. 'You want a slap?'

The pair had been best mates since nursery school, but that didn't mean Zhang wouldn't get physical if George mouthed off.

Greg tried to prick the tension. 'You're such a

pair of tarts,' he sneered. 'Go on, snog and make up like you always do.'

Zhang took a step back before turning around and staring Greg out, but he wouldn't have dared do anything: Greg was only average height for a Year Eight, but he was sturdy and biceps bulged under his rolled-up shirt sleeves.

'Oh Greg, I forgot,' George said, as he scooped the last of the junk in his locker into the open mouth of his backpack. 'I'm getting dragged to some barbecue at my aunt's house on Saturday, Zhang's flying off to China on Sunday – so if we're gonna have the X-box sleepover, I'm afraid it's tonight or not at all.'

'Oh,' Greg said awkwardly, running his hand through a tangle of dark hair.

'You can still come, right?' George asked.

Greg shrugged, pulling a little Nokia out of his pocket. 'Sure, I guess. I mean . . . I'll just text my dad to make sure, but there's nothing else going on, so I can't see why not.'

'Cool,' George said, slamming the door of his locker before wiping his brow on his sleeve.

'I take it my cousin Andy can still come?' Greg

asked. 'I know you've never met him, but he's the biggest laugh, I swear.'

'More the merrier, I say,' George answered, before making a big huffing sound. 'I don't mind the sun, but it's just *too* hot today!'

Greg laughed. 'This is nothing. When I lived in Australia you'd get days like this in *winter*.'

Zhang tried to copy Greg's Australian accent. 'When I lived in Auuuuuustralia it was four hundred degrees in the shade. It was so hot the koala bears dropped out of the trees ready-cooked.'

'Don't mock the accent,' Greg smirked. 'It drives the chicks wild.'

'No accounting for female tastes,' Zhang said. 'The meat-heads they go out with . . .'

'Just because Amy blew you out twice,' George grinned, as he strolled towards the window.

'Oh and you're *such* a stud,' Zhang replied.

George stood on the chair by the window and leaned out to cool off in the breeze. He heard a distinctive laugh in the playground below and looked straight down.

George turned back inside. 'Zhang!' he yelled eagerly. 'Gimme that coleslaw. My sister's standing *right* under this window.'

Greg and Zhang rushed over, dragging chairs behind them.

'Nice,' Zhang grinned, as the three boys leaned out and stared down into the sunny playground. 'Your sister's *so* fit.'

'Eww,' George shuddered. 'You wouldn't fancy her if *you'd* seen her in the bath, shaving her hairy-arsed legs.'

'Face facts,' Greg said, shaking his head. 'If Sophie was anything other than your fifteen-year-old sister you'd be perving at her the same as everyone else.'

'It's personality that counts,' George noted. 'And she's a grade-one pain in the butthole.'

'You know what I don't get?' Greg said, looking across at Zhang. 'How does George, with his Twiglet arms and legs, get to have a *total* babe for a sister?'

'Shut up,' George ordered.

Greg and Zhang did shut up. Not because George had told them, but because he'd popped the lid off Zhang's tub of eight-month-old coleslaw.

'That's *so* rank,' Greg moaned.

'It's bubbling,' George said, trying not to breathe. 'The tub is actually warm!'

'Lob it then,' Zhang said impatiently. 'What are you waiting for?'

Greg looked across and saw doubt all over George's face.

'Do it,' Zhang urged. 'Remember: Sophie lent her ex-boyfriend half your PSP games and you never got 'em back.'

George shook his head and moved to put the lid back on the pot. 'Better not. If my old lady found out she'd make a misery of my whole summer holidays.'

'You chicken!' Zhang tutted. 'I *knew* you'd bottle it.'

As George lined up the lid to pop it back on, Zhang reached over and batted his arm. The coleslaw shot up out of George's hand. He tried catching it but the pot glanced off his fingertips and headed for the ground.

Greg looked down and got a surprise: Sophie and her gaggle of mates had scattered to avoid a football rifling across from the adjacent Astroturf.

'Watch where you're kicking that, you knob!' Sophie shouted.

George, Zhang and Greg watched open mouthed as a bare-chested Year-Ten boy charged in to grab the football. The tension made it feel like slow motion: Sophie and her friends moving away, the coleslaw pot spinning in the air and the beefy Year Ten running in to retrieve the ball.

'Zhang you *idiot!*' George gasped.

The tub of rancid coleslaw hit the Year Ten's neck as he scooped the football off the concrete. The brown mass erupted, spattering down his bare back and up as far as the top of his shaven head.

Upstairs, the three boys dived away from the window, but in his haste George forgot to duck and whacked the back of his head on the frame.

'You moron!' George shouted to Zhang, as he jumped down off the chair. 'That was Thomas Moran. If he finds us we're dead.'

'Who's Thomas Moran when he's out shopping?' Greg asked.

George anxiously rubbed the bump on the back of his head. 'Just one of the hardest kids in Year

Ten, that's all. Him and his mates are all rugby players. *Big* rugby players.'

'Maybe they didn't see us,' Greg suggested. 'They might not even know what window it was thrown from.'

Zhang crept up to the window and peeked out. 'They saw us!' he gasped, before ducking back down. 'Sophie and all her mates are pointing up. Moran and another big dude are sprinting towards the main entrance.'

George was waving his bandy arms around, working himself into a complete state. 'Why did you hit my arm you idiot? Those guys aren't gonna take prisoners. If they catch us, they'll kick our heads in.'

Greg swept his backpack off his desk and headed for the door. 'Less panic, more running,' he suggested.

'This is so bad,' George shuddered.

As Zhang belted outside into the corridor Greg grabbed George by his collar and yanked him towards the door.

'Calm down, you'll be OK,' Greg said. 'But we've got to start running, *now*.'

By the time George and Greg got out into the hallway, Zhang had already made it to the main staircase, thirty metres away. He'd hoped to get down to the first floor and hide out in a classroom there, but he had no chance because the two big Year Tens were already bounding up from the ground floor.

'There's the fat one!' Thomas Moran shouted. 'You wait till I get my hands on you.'

Zhang's shoes squealed on the corridor tiles as he saw Greg and George belting out of the classroom in the opposite direction.

'Guys,' Zhang yelled desperately, running as fast his chunky legs would allow. 'Guys, wait up!'

2. LAKE

The British countryside is dotted with secret government installations: nuclear research facilities, weapons dumps, communications monitoring centres. CHERUB campus was in the highest security category, surrounded by government-owned forest and marked on maps as an artillery firing range.

Anyone ignoring the warning signs and driving up the approach road towards campus' solid black gates would be greeted by guards armed with Heckler and Koch machine guns. You couldn't even view campus from the air because the sky overhead formed part of the protected airspace around a military airbase five kilometres to the east.

If you *had* been allowed to overfly CHERUB campus you'd have seen a set of buildings similar to those you'd find at a wealthy boarding school, surrounded by sports pitches and outdoor tennis courts. More unusual were a banana-shaped building bristling with satellite dishes, four helipads and beyond a large oval lake a wooded area, containing an assault course and an outdoor shooting range.

The weather was glorious and more than half the kids on CHERUB campus had taken their lunch outside to eat by the lake. Some kids cooled off with a paddle, but swimming was presently banned because it might disturb the family of ducklings living on a muddy embankment near the lake's centre.

Twelve-year-old Lauren Adams lay on the lawn near the lake's edge, toes curled in the grass, surrounded by daisies and using her arm to keep the sun out of her eyes. She'd managed to get her favourite sushi box from the canteen before they ran out and the sun made her whole body feel wonderfully warm, but she was still depressed because she was in trouble and it wasn't her fault.

A fair-skinned boy called Andy Lagan sat on the grass next to Lauren. He put his Manga down and tapped her arm. 'Zara's here,' he said grimly. 'Better start putting your boots on.'

Lauren wanted time to freeze so she could stay on the warm grass for ever. 'God,' she moaned, sweeping blades of grass off her soles as she sat up.

All cherubs wore a military style uniform during school hours: a T-shirt with CHERUB logo – the colour of which depended upon your rank – olive combat trousers with zip-off legs and lightweight black boots. As Andy pulled his grey T-shirt over his chest and started moving uphill, Lauren hurriedly pulled balled-up socks out of her boots.

'You'd better shift,' Andy shouted back at her. 'Zara's gonna be in a right mood.'

Zara Asker stood on a tarmac path fifty metres uphill. She had one hand on her hip and leaned on one of the electric carts that staff used to move around campus. Zara was thirty-seven years old; she wore a flower-print dress and still carried some of the weight from the birth of her second child a year earlier.

Belying her mumsy appearance, Zara held one of

the most senior jobs in British Intelligence. As the chairwoman of CHERUB, she was a headteacher and a spymaster rolled into one. Zara was usually popular with the kids in her charge, except when it was time to dish out punishments.

Lauren rushed to join Andy and six other CHERUB agents up on the path, with her boot laces dragging behind her. There was a boy and girl in their early teens, but the main clump comprised four grey-shirt boys aged ten and eleven. They were all mates and their unelected leader was the spiky-haired Jake Parker.

'Right you lot, line up,' Zara said stiffly, before eyeballing Jake's soggy trousers and ketchup-stained shirt. 'Is *that* how you present yourself to the chairwoman?'

Lauren couldn't stand Jake and enjoyed his discomfort as he hurriedly tucked in his shirt. 'Sorry, Miss,' Jake said meekly. 'I dropped my hot dog.'

Zara zoomed in and inspected the stain. 'Make sure you soak the shirt in detergent before you take it down to the laundry.'

'Yes, Miss,' Jake nodded. Zara could be a bit random when she dished out punishments and the eleven-year-old was relieved to have received nothing more than laundry advice.

But the chairwoman hadn't finished with them yet. 'Before I start, have any of you got anything you want to say?' Zara asked.

The eight uniformed agents looked sheepish and tried to avoid catching the chairwoman's gaze. Lauren wanted to say that it was Jake and his three mates who'd caused all the trouble, but she was smart enough to know that it would only make things worse: Jake would throw the accusation right back at her and it would descend into a slanging match that would make Zara even madder.

Zara adjusted the strap of her summer dress and gave a deep sigh. 'You eight are all qualified CHERUB agents,' she said. 'From black shirts like Lauren to some of you younger boys who are still awaiting your first mission. But no kid gets inside CHERUB campus unless you're from the brightest two or three per cent of the population. Then we put you through the wringer: language training, espionage training, combat training and physical training. In other words, the eight of you are amongst the most outstandingly capable people of your age anywhere in the world. And that's why I'm so disgusted by what happened this morning.'

Zara reached inside the electric buggy and retrieved a crumpled paper aeroplane from the passenger seat. It was made from a giant sheet of cartridge paper. It had *I'm So Bored Airlines* written along the side and a crudely drawn penis on the tail.

'This was just one of eleven paper darts I found in that classroom. Along with hundreds of paper balls, boot-prints all over the tabletops and damage to a Venetian blind where some idiot appears to have tried to swing off it.'

Lauren struggled not to smile: one of the few high points of her morning had been watching Jake trying to recover a paper aeroplane stuck up high between the blind slats, only to crash off the tabletop and bang his head on the window ledge while desperately grabbing at the blind to save himself.

Zara continued, 'What makes this worse is that you behaved like this in front of a guest speaker. I *know* it's hard to concentrate when it's as hot as today, and perhaps a ninety-minute lecture on preserving DNA evidence isn't particularly exciting. But Mr Donaldson travelled all the way up from MI5 headquarters in London to speak with you and I assumed you were all mature enough to behave yourselves without a staff member looking over your shoulder.'

Andy raised his hand tentatively. 'Miss, not all of us were involved.'

Zara's eyes bulged. 'I saw the size of the boot-prints on the desktops, Andy. Mr Donaldson made it clear that the four younger boys were primarily responsible, but none of you four older kids intervened. Even if you didn't think you could control the situation yourselves, you could have walked down the hall to another classroom and brought the situation to the attention of a staff member. You're trained CHERUB agents. How can you expect to be sent out on missions to fight terrorists and drug dealers when you haven't even got the brainpower to deal with a couple of lads getting out of hand during a lecture?'

Lauren was irritated by these comments. Zara had once been a CHERUB agent herself, but she'd clearly forgotten the unwritten rule that cherubs didn't grass each other up.

'You're all getting identical punishments,' Zara announced. 'Seven pounds fifty pocket money deducted to pay for the damaged blind and you're going to be spending the rest of this sunny afternoon doing physical training on the assault course with Miss Speaks.'

The eight cherubs groaned, but only Jake was dumb enough to mouth off.

'That's bull,' he yelled. 'When was the last time people had to run the assault course just for messing in class? Laps of the athletic track maybe . . .'

Zara swooped down so that she was looking Jake straight in the eye. 'You mucked around in front of a campus guest, causing me personal embarassment. Outside lecturers are a vital part of your ongoing training and they won't want to come here if you behave like that, will they?'

'No, Miss,' Jake said, adopting a surly *if you say so* voice.

'I don't like your tone, Jake Parker,' Zara said, now getting really angry. 'Seeing as you're so keen on punishment laps, you can also run twenty a day for the next week. Your smart mouth also just cost you an extra month's pocket money and got you grounded in your room for the next two weekends.'

Jake's head shrivelled between his shoulders. Lauren enjoyed seeing him suffer: it seemed like the least Jake deserved after costing her seven fifty and an afternoon of gruelling training on the assault course.

'Miss Speaks is waiting,' Zara shouted, pointing dramatically towards the wooded area beyond the lake. 'All of you start running to the training compound before I *really* lose my temper.'

3. MOVES

'Move it,' Greg shouted, grabbing George by his collar.

'I can't,' George gasped. 'Got a stitch.'

They'd run down the long second-floor corridor and on to the back stairs, which were off limits to pupils unless there was a fire drill. Zhang was overweight and kept falling further behind, while the two Year Tens closed relentlessly.

Greg gave George another pull, tugging him off the landing. 'Through the sixth-form block and we'll be in the canteen,' Greg explained. 'They won't be able to touch us in there: it's full of teachers.'

The sense of hope gave George some energy and

he leaned over the banister and started moving down as quickly as he could.

'You're so unfit,' Greg moaned. 'You should take up jogging or something.'

Zhang had caught up by the time they'd reached the bottom of the staircase, but Thomas Moran and his mate Johno were now just a single flight of stairs behind them.

Greg turned left towards the sixth-form annexe, but he was horrified to find the doors locked. Through the safety glass he saw the soft chairs and furniture all piled up and white sheets spread over the carpet tiles. A sign on the door spelled their doom:

The sixth-form block is getting a lick of paint!
Reopens September 2007
Have a great summer!!!!

'Dammit,' Greg shouted.

'We're puppy food,' George gasped.

Out of options, Zhang led the trio back towards the staircase. Thomas Moran had reached the bottom, but Zhang used his bulk to plough through and start running down the short corridor that led to the sports hall.

The floor was covered with dried-out mud trailed in from the playing fields and the air smelled like BO. The corridor ended at a T-junction, with double doors leading into the gymnasium directly ahead, a pink corridor leading left to the girls' changing room and a blue one going towards the boys'.

The gym was always locked at lunchtime and Zhang shoulder-charging the doors made no difference to that. The smell grew even worse as they reached the boys' changing rooms. The air was steamy and rogue pieces of kit scattered the puddled floor. There was a communal shower at one end and a putrid-smelling toilet block at the other.

Greg and George ran in and headed towards the showers. They'd been in here a hundred times before but they glanced around, hoping against hope that there was a fire door or some other exit they'd never noticed before.

'Dead end, boys,' Thomas Moran whooped, smashing his huge fist into his palm as Zhang slammed the door of a toilet cubicle and bolted himself in.

'Be reasonable,' George begged, holding out his hands as he backed up to the showers with Greg. 'It was meant for my sister. If you let me off I'll pay you twenty pounds, first day of next term. I swear on my life.'

At the opposite end of the room, Johno's size-ten Nike blasted the cubicle door, not only breaking the lock, but ripping off the hinges on the opposite side too. Zhang howled with pain as the door crashed down on his head.

'*Heeeeeere's* Johno!' Johno grinned, throwing the door out of the cubicle before laying into Zhang with hard punches. 'Guess where I'm gonna stick your head!'

As Zhang screamed for mercy, Greg pushed George back towards the showers and faced off Thomas Moran. Greg was tough looking, but one of the youngest in his year and only just about to turn thirteen. Thomas was bigger in every direction and his cropped hair and the sweat streaking down his muscular torso made him look fearsome.

'You're a cool guy,' Thomas sneered. 'Why you hanging out with a fat freak and a skinny freak anyway?'

'I don't want any trouble,' Greg said diplomatically. 'But I'm warning you, my dad's a kickboxing instructor. I know how to handle myself.'

Thomas laughed so hard that he showered Greg with spit. 'Bring it on, titch. Show us your moves!'

In the background Zhang screamed out as Johno dunked his face into the toilet bowl and pulled the flush.

Thomas turned back and saw Zhang on his knees, with Johno's whole weight pressing down on his back.

'Nice one, Johno,' Thomas jeered. 'I reckon these two could do with a hair wash as well.'

Greg twisted back around his left shoulder and pulled his hand up tight above his wrist. As Thomas turned back Greg thrust upwards, smashing the palm of his hand against Thomas' temple.

Thomas Moran's neck snapped around so fast that his eyeballs didn't have time to follow. George recoiled in horror as he watched Thomas crash backwards into the changing-room wall with nothing but pure white in his eyeballs. Unconscious, the beefy Year Ten slid down the wall at a weird angle, ending up with his legs splayed out and his torso lying across the changing bench.

'Jesus!' George gasped. 'What have you done?'

Greg didn't answer because he'd stepped over Thomas' legs and headed confidently past the rows of hooks and into the toilet block. It was a nasty space: mud and piss all over the floor, broken sinks and a smell you didn't even want to think about.

It would have been difficult for Greg to pull Johno out of the cubicle. Luckily, Johno turned to see his pal Thomas slumped on the floor and charged forwards with both fists swinging. Greg ducked, then bobbed up and drove a punch hard into Johno's nose.

Caught off guard, Johno stumbled back as Greg launched a devastating assault. His blows hit all the weak spots: a dig in the ribs, two knees in the kidneys and a final chop behind the neck that sent Johno sprawling.

Johno ended up on the rank floor, clutching hands over his bloody nose. Zhang staggered out of the cubicle, his shirt drenched and toilet water streaking down his face. Greg let him deliver a single kick in revenge for the bog-washing before pulling him back.

'Johno's had enough,' Greg smiled. 'You OK, Zhang?'

Zhang had taken a beating and his voice trembled. 'That toilet was nasty.'

'You've got bus fare,' Greg said. 'Go home, take a shower. You'll only miss half of first lesson and we'll cover for you.'

Over on the floor near the urinals, Johno was coughing and trying to find his feet.

Greg pointed Johno's way and snarled, 'You stay down until we've left.'

As Zhang headed out George came over from the changing area where he'd been nervously inspecting Thomas Moran.

'I think he's alive,' George said.

'He'll be fine,' Greg replied. 'Little tap on the temple never killed anyone. He'll have concussion and a nice headache to remember me by.'

'We'd better get out of here,' George said. 'If someone sees this . . .'

'Just gimme a sec,' Greg said, grabbing a horrible grey sliver of soap stuck on the side of the only working sink and turning on the tap. 'Can't walk around with your blood all over my fists, can I Johno?'

Johno had a rugby player's build and was nearly six feet tall, but he'd propped himself against the wall and was fighting back tears.

Greg dried his hands on his trousers as George followed him out into the corridor.

'What if Johno grasses you?' George asked anxiously.

'Yeah right,' Greg smiled. 'They're both twice my size. Who's gonna believe that story?'

'I wouldn't believe it myself if I hadn't seen with my own eyes,' George gushed. 'I owe you, man. I thought I was gonna get serious beats. I know you said you knew some kickboxing moves, but I never knew you were *that* good. Usually when people brag about being a black belt or some crap like that it's all made up . . .'

'My dad's an instructor,' Greg said. 'I practise

every day after school.'

'Awesome,' George said. 'Nobody's gonna give us any hassle once this story spreads around.'

Greg smiled coyly as they rounded the bottom of the staircase, heading back to their second-floor form room. He'd lied about his dad, a man who'd really died in Australia fifteen months earlier and had never kickboxed in his life.

Greg's full name was Gregory Rathbone, but the other agents on CHERUB campus always called him Rat.

4. PUNISHMENT

The assault course on CHERUB campus was a two-kilometre circuit, complete with rat-infested tunnels, rope swings, climbing walls, jagged rocks and a fast-flowing stream. A normal twelve-year-old might complete the course in an hour, although the chances are they'd fail at least one obstacle because of some weakness – like being scared of heights, not having enough strength to swing over the hanging bars, or good enough balance to cross the narrow beams.

But the eight kids Zara Asker sent for punishment had all completed the course hundreds of times during their basic training. Andy Lagan and Lauren Adams both had personal-best assault course times below twenty minutes. They still found running the course exhausting, but they could handle it and it certainly didn't satisfy Instructor Speaks' definition of a punishment.

Miss Speaks was the kind of woman you didn't want to get on the wrong side of. Her shoulders were huge, her voice boomed like she'd swallowed a megaphone and she was particularly proud of her massive arms, which enabled her to beat everyone on campus at arm wrestling, including all of the male training instructors.

To make the assault course tougher, Speaks gave the eight kids backpacks containing ten to fifteen kilos of lead plates, depending upon their age and height. Between the obstacles, she'd marked out exercise stations where the agents had to perform squats, crunches, jumping jacks or whatever. And as if that wasn't enough, the assault course was fitted with traps which made the course more difficult if someone was on hand to operate them.

The course started with a run up a fifty-metre slope. In places it was so steep that you had to use rocks as footholds and haul yourself up lengths of knotted rope. If you got this wrong you'd roll down to the bottom if you were lucky, or split your head open on a rock if you weren't.

The top of this hill was the highest part of the assault course, from which an instructor could survey the entire training compound. After a short run over flat ground were three long beams placed two metres apart. At ten centimetres wide, crossing them didn't require exceptional balance, but you needed some nerve because after the first few steps the ground dropped away and you found yourself suspended above a stagnant pool surrounded by beds of stinging nettles.

Some of the older agents on campus worked as assistants to the training instructors. Fifteen-year-old James Adams had snapped up the chance to escape double History and help Miss Speaks out, especially as he'd spent the previous evening on his PlayStation instead of writing his essay on Napoleon.

James sat on a wooden platform suspended between two oak trees which overlooked the narrow beams. His mate Bruce Norris squatted a couple of metres away, while in between were two red punchbags, suspended from a sturdy branch in the canopy above.

In the distance James and Bruce heard kids grunting as they hauled themselves up the slope, while Miss Speaks leaned over the edge taunting them.

'Move it, brats!' Speaks bellowed, as she kicked a clump of dry earth down the slope on to the trainees. 'Grab that rope and heave . . . You call that heaving? You'd *better* put some oomph in unless you want your butts enrolled on a two-month after-school fitness programme.'

James smirked as his sister Lauren's head emerged over the top of the slope. The assault course was easier if you worked with a partner and Andy was just a couple of steps behind her. The pair were starting their third circuit out of four and the hot weather was doing them in.

Lauren's face was bright red and sweat streamed out of her tied-back hair. Andy's grey shirt had dark sweat patches under the arms, while their trousers and bare arms were encrusted with filth after crawling through the tunnel and wading across a muddy stream basin.

'Push-ups,' Speaks screamed. 'I want twenty-five. Don't gawp like a pair of prunes. Move, move, move!'

James watched as his sister and Andy hit the ground. Lauren was stocky and easily knocked off twenty-five push-ups, despite having twelve and a half kilos of lead on her back. Andy's skinny arms were not only weaker than Lauren's, they were gangly – meaning he had to move a lot further to complete each push-up. After fifteen his arms gave out.

'What the hell is that?' Speaks demanded. 'Call yourself a man? Your girlfriend's tougher than you.'

Andy tried to make a sixteenth push-up – he was in good shape and could manage forty when he hadn't just completed two circuits of the assault course on the hottest day of the year – but his shoulders ached and his arms shuddered before collapsing back to the hot earth.

'You're so weak,' Speaks shouted, as she planted her size-eleven boot on the back of Andy's head. 'You're a mealy little worm. What are you?'

Andy found it hard to speak because his lips

were squished in the dirt. 'Mweely lwttle worm,' he gasped.

'Wriggle like a worm then,' Speaks shouted.

Humiliated, Andy wriggled his hips and flailed his arms in the dirt. Lauren scowled furiously at the instructor.

'Are you eyeballing me, sister?' Speaks shouted. 'Why don't you abandon him? What use is this little worm to you?'

'He's my partner,' Lauren said loyally.

'Tell you what,' Speaks said, sounding like she'd just had the greatest idea in history. 'He's ten short. How about you get down in the dirt and do 'em for him?'

Lauren didn't like it, but she wanted the instructor out of her sight so she hit the dirt and started counting Andy's press-ups. Her lead-filled pack was chafing all the skin on her back, she was boiling hot, her arms hurt and sweat dripped off the end of her nose into the dirt.

Strict discipline, tough punishments and hard physical training were the three worst things about being a CHERUB agent, but they gave cherubs an edge that enabled them to work safely undercover and accomplish tasks well beyond the scope of ordinary kids.

There was nothing to stop Lauren or any other agent quitting campus and going to live an ordinary life with a foster family, but even when her lungs burned and her boots were full of blisters she never considered it. Because when you showered off, patched up your wounds and looked in the mirror you saw an extraordinary person looking back at you.

Three years earlier, Lauren had arrived on campus as a bright but perfectly ordinary nine-year-old. Now she was one of the most highly rated agents on CHERUB campus. She spoke fluent Spanish and Russian, was fit enough to run ten kilometres without getting out of breath, could handle a car on a skid pan, load and shoot any firearm you cared to name and if she couldn't get her hands on a weapon she also knew several ways to kill you with her bare hands.

As Lauren made the tenth and final upwards push, Miss Speaks' enormous hand pressed down against her pack. The harder Lauren fought to straighten her arms, the more Speaks pushed against them.

'Back-chatting a guest on campus,' Speaks tutted. 'Are you regretting it now, you vile little tramp?'

Lauren tried not to think about how this was all Jake Parker's fault as she gritted her teeth and stared at the dirt. Sweat was now pouring down her face and her stomach muscles felt like they were going to explode, but failure wasn't an option: Miss Speaks would only devise some other form of torture.

Lauren finally came close to getting her arms straight, but Speaks shoved downwards and Lauren found her nose back in the dirt and grit sticking to her sweaty face. In basic training cherubs are taught to shut out pain and focus on a seven-word mantra: *This is tough but cherubs are tougher.* Lauren closed her eyes and silently mouthed it to herself.

Finally, after almost a minute of straining, Miss Speaks released her grip and Lauren completed the push-up.

'Determined,' Speaks said admiringly, as Lauren staggered to her feet. 'You've got heart.'

Compliments from training instructors were as rare as chicks hatching from Cadbury's Creme Eggs. Lauren grudgingly acknowledged the compliment as she straightened up. The heat made her woozy and her eyes moved in different directions as she looked ahead.

'Move off then,' Speaks yelled. 'Across those beams before my boot comes swiftly into contact with your little pink arses.'

'You OK?' Andy asked guiltily as they staggered towards the beams. 'Sorry. I'm *so* bad at push-ups.'

Lauren shrugged. 'Not your fault God gave you weedy arms.'

James and Bruce watched from the platform in the trees as Lauren and Andy each lined up at the start of a beam. As Lauren stepped off, Bruce reached up and dropped a bar that held the punchbags in place. James and Bruce each grabbed a leather handle stitched to the back of a bag and lined up behind them.

'I'll go for Lauren,' James said.

Because Lauren had done his push-ups, Andy felt fresher and moved off faster. Lauren could have done with a moment to catch her breath and wipe the grit off her face, but she knew Speaks would bite her head off if she showed any sign of slacking.

As Andy took his third step, Bruce gave his heavy bag an almighty shove towards him. James and Bruce's platform was disguised by the trees and the first thing Andy knew about their presence was when the rope holding up the bag creaked and the huge leather sack sliced across his path just a few centimetres in front of him.

'Missed,' Bruce cursed, reaching out to catch the bag as it swung back towards the platform.

James released his bag. He didn't always get on with his sister, but he had no desire to knock her into a muddy pond so he swung the bag out wide, missing her by several metres.

'James Adams,' Miss Speaks shouted furiously. 'If I see you going soft like that again I'll have *you* running this assault course tomorrow.'

Andy should have cleared the beam already, but it takes a few seconds to compose yourself after you stop and Bruce's second shot came around in a circular arc. The bag smashed into Andy just as he got his balance back and started moving again.

'Bull's-eye!' Bruce shouted triumphantly.

As Lauren made a three-metre jump on to the muddy crash-mat at the end of her beam, Andy clattered through a canopy of overhanging branches and hit the pond below. After a big splash, Andy grabbed a branch and hauled himself out of the brown soup, but as he lunged forward a horrific pain shot down his chest, making him cry out.

The water was two metres deep and the bottom of the pond had a cushioned lining to prevent serious accidents, but Andy's face was screwed up in agony as he staggered towards the embankment. James and Bruce climbed down the rope ladder from their platform, then held their bare arms up high as they navigated the tangle of stinging nettles surrounding the water.

'What are you whinging about, Lagan?' James asked.

'Cracked rib or something,' Andy gasped. 'It's absolute agony, all down my right side.'

Up above, Jake Parker and his mate Ewan had made it up the slope at the start of their third circuit. They didn't get push-ups because Miss Speaks was looking down at Andy and they didn't get hit by the heavy bags because James and Bruce were guiding him through the stinging nettles.

Jake grinned at Lauren when he jumped off the

beam, with Ewan coming off the next beam a few steps behind.

'Looks like it's our lucky day,' Jake chirped, giving Lauren a cheeky wink. 'What happened to your boyfriend?'

Lauren was sick of Jake and this was more than she could take. She made sure Miss Speaks wasn't looking before grabbing Jake's earlobe and twisting hard.

'First off, he's not my boyfriend,' Lauren growled. 'Second, if you'd behaved this morning I'd be sitting in a nice air-conditioned Art class right now. So stop smiling and start walking, because I'm this close to kicking the snot out of you.'

'I'm *so* scared of you,' Jake taunted, but only after Lauren had let go and he was well out of range.

On the opposite side of the lake Miss Speaks stared down at the three boys. 'Is he really hurt?' she asked suspiciously.

'Looks like it,' Bruce shouted up, as two more boys raced across the beams overhead.

Speaks shook her head and sighed dramatically. 'OK, James, you take the little worm to the medical unit and get him looked at. But I'm gonna be checking in with Dr Kessler, Andy. If you're faking, I'll have you back here for a special one-on-one training session that'll make this seem like a Buckingham Palace garden party.'

5. CASCADE

CHERUB campus has a small medical centre with six private rooms and a five-bed casualty ward. Andy lay at the far end of the well equipped ward, while an eight-year-old who'd burned her hand on a cake tin sat at the other end feeling sorry for herself.

Andy sat up, wincing with pain, as two men came through the swing doors. They were similar in appearance, with bald heads and silver-framed glasses. One was Dr Kessler, who Andy had been expecting for almost an hour. The other man was the mission controller John Jones, who he wasn't expecting at all.

Kessler had worked on campus for more than

twenty years, but his German accent never faltered.

'Good news, I think,' he said, reaching across Andy's bed and peeling off his covers to examine his chest. 'I checked the X-ray and there's no break, but you've got some nice bruises coming up. I just want you to try raising your left shoulder off the pillow.'

Andy barely lifted his shoulder before he hissed with pain and slumped back on to his pillow.

Dr Kessler looked at John Jones. 'He's pulled a muscle. It's probably the most common injury I see: the kids train hard and muscle is much more susceptible to damage when heavily fatigued.'

Andy looked at Dr Kessler. 'But I should be OK for my mission on Saturday, shouldn't I?'

John cut Andy off. 'I had a text message from Greg Rathbone about ninety minutes ago. George Lydon has to visit his aunt's house on Saturday, so he's moved the sleepover forward to tonight.'

'Damn,' Andy tutted.

'Why didn't you tell Zara that you had an important mission coming up?' John asked.

'I didn't want Lauren and them to think I was trying to wheedle out of it,' Andy explained.

'Is anyone else on campus trained to use AutoCAD software?'

John shook his head. 'You've had over twenty hours' training, there's no way we can get anyone up to your standard by this evening.'

'Strap me up and I'll get through it somehow,' Andy said bravely. 'I'll just tell everyone I got hurt playing football or something.'

'I can get Nurse Halstead to apply some strapping,' Dr Kessler nodded. 'But you'd still be in a significant amount of pain. A painkilling injection would help, although the injection is intra-muscular so it will hurt, and the affected area will feel quite peculiar; the same kind of numb feeling you get after a filling at the dentist.'

'The choice is entirely yours, Andy,' John emphasised. 'You don't have to put yourself through this. If you pull out of the mission nobody will hold it against you.'

Andy shook his head determinedly. 'Rat's been trying to get us into Kurt Lydon's house for over a month. I'll do what it takes.'

Dr Kessler headed back across the ward and unlocked a wheeled rubber cabinet, fitted with hundreds of tiny drawers. John pulled a wodge of paperwork out of his jacket.

'It'll take about ninety minutes to drive to Milton Keynes,' John said. 'And I want to get on the road before the kids get out of school. So I need you to go through your mission background document and the detailed briefing. If you've got any questions now's the time to ask.'

Andy took the papers and shrugged. 'I've read all this twenty times already.'

'I know,' John nodded. 'But I'm always paranoid that my agents will forget something at the last minute. Do me a favour and give it a final once-over, OK?'

Andy nodded reluctantly as Dr Kessler headed back holding a sterile syringe pack.

'This should be good for twelve to sixteen hours,' Kessler said. 'But remember that the muscle underneath is still damaged. You've got to avoid doing anything too physical.'

After swabbing Andy's chest with a sterile wipe, the doctor ripped the plastic wrapping from the syringe pack and twisted off a plastic bung, unveiling a long needle.

'Bloody hell!' Andy gasped. 'Is that going to hurt as much as I think it's going to?'

'Oh, it's ten times worse than it looks,' Dr Kessler said sarcastically. 'Just take deep breaths and keep still. It'll only take a few moments.'

Andy let go of John's paperwork and dug his nails into the mattress as the needle pierced his stomach.

*

CLASSIFIED MISSION BACKGROUND DOCUMENT
FOR GREG 'RAT' RATHBONE & ANDY LAGAN DO <u>NOT</u> PHOTOCOPY OR MAKE NOTES

MISSION BACKGROUND – THE NUCLEAR CLUB
Since the United States detonated the first atomic bombs in 1945 many other countries have attempted to build their own nuclear weapons. At present eight other countries are known to possess nuclear weapons (Russia, United Kingdom, France, China, India, Pakistan, North Korea and Israel) while others such as Japan and Germany have nuclear technology but have chosen not to make bombs.

For every country that has nuclear weapons there

are many more that want them. Some of these countries are poor and have no realistic chances of developing a nuclear arsenal. Others, particularly in the oil-rich Middle East, are wealthy but lack the scientific and industrial base needed to develop them.

These countries will pay huge sums of money to anyone who can supply them with nuclear secrets.

THE DARK SUN NETWORK

Over the past sixty years many groups and individuals have tried to cash in on the market for nuclear technology. In 2004 a joint operation between British and French intelligence officers led to the arrest of a woman who'd illegally purchased several tonnes of maraging steel. This specially hardened metal is mainly used in the nuclear industry and its production and export is strictly controlled.

Facing a lengthy prison term, the suspect agreed to cooperate. She gave the French intelligence service valuable information on a criminal organisation known as Dark Sun. Over the following months it became clear that Dark Sun was a sophisticated network that bought and sold secret nuclear technology. Its customers included governments in Africa, Asia and the Middle East.

THE CASCADE

The most difficult part of producing a nuclear bomb is turning ordinary uranium metal into the weapons grade variety needed to fuel a bomb. This is done by heating the metal until it becomes a gas and spinning it at very high speed in a centrifuge.

To make weapons grade material, uranium gas needs to be passed through a network of up to fifty thousand centrifuges known as a cascade. Not only is a cascade hugely complex, but it also uses the electricity output of a large power station and any leak or malfunction will lead to the release of deadly radioactive gas.

KURT LYDON

The Dark Sun network wants to offer its customers reliable designs for uranium centrifuges. Several European and Chinese centrifuge designs are widely available, but these all date from the 1960s and 70s. Their performance and safety is well below that of the best modern equipment.

Kurt Lydon was part of a legitimate engineering team designing a new Anglo-French uranium centrifuge. By November 2006 the design was complete and a small cascade had been successfully tested, but the

French government cancelled a planned uranium enrichment plant. The centrifuge project was canned and Kurt Lydon was out of a job.

Despite the high security surrounding any nuclear project, Lydon managed to steal the computerised blueprints for the new centrifuge shortly before he was laid off. The theft went undetected, but MI5 identified Lydon when he met with a suspected Dark Sun operative in a Brussels restaurant in February 2007.

Over the following weeks, MI5 bugged Lydon's home and all of his telephone conversations. Lydon was trying to sell the centrifuge design to the Dark Sun network for eight million euros. But the new design required sophisticated metal composites, bearings and motors that are subject to strict export controls.

Dark Sun might have been able to smuggle enough of these components to build a test centrifuge, but it would be impossible to get hold of enough specialised material for the fifty thousand needed in a cascade.

Lydon was disappointed that his state-of-the-art design was of no value to the Dark Sun network. However, he received a more positive response when he offered to redesign the centrifuge so that it could be built from simpler components and materials.

Lydon estimates that his redesign work will take eight to ten months. MI5 has considered arresting Lydon and his contacts. This might provide some intelligence, but only with junior members of the Dark Sun network.

MI5 wants to penetrate the highest levels of Dark Sun. The only way to do this is to allow Lydon to complete his redesign and then track his progress as he travels abroad to build and test it. However, if Lydon is successful, his easy-to-build centrifuge could enable dozens of countries to start making fuel for nuclear bombs.

MI5 has contacted some of Lydon's former colleagues. The centrifuge design contains over three thousand parts and nobody understands all of them. The engineers selected a list of four hundred key parts. These are all made from common materials, meaning Lydon would have no reason to alter their design or to examine them too closely.

Once the engineers had their list, they began to think up minute changes to these parts that would affect their performance. In a centrifuge spinning at 25,000rpm a hundredth of a gram imbalance in weight can cause a catastrophic failure; the wrong type of plastic seal can create an explosive venting of gas; or a tiny imperfection in the centrifuge lining can cause a heat build-up that makes the entire unit explode.

A failed centrifuge is likely to spread radioactive debris, but experts believe that contamination will be confined to a small area. Engineers and technicians working for Dark Sun may come to serious harm, but MI5 feels this risk is acceptable, given that millions of lives would be endangered if a rogue state or terrorist group obtained a nuclear bomb.

The engineers studied the individual parts and honed their list down to 143 tiny design alterations that will be unnoticeable on a computer screen and impossible to pinpoint in the aftermath of an explosion.

It is believed that ironing out all of these tiny faults will actually take longer than designing a new centrifuge from scratch. Testing the flawed design will also take years, cost millions of dollars and undermine the credibility of the Dark Sun network.

THE PROBLEM
Kurt Lydon has already begun work on his revised design. Someone will have to access the computer-aided design workstation in the study at Kurt Lydon's

Milton Keynes home and enter all 143 design alterations by hand.

MI5 believed this would be a relatively simple matter of disabling Lydon's burglar alarm and breaking in, but the Dark Sun network is keeping a close eye on Kurt Lydon and has his home under twenty-four-hour surveillance.

No adult operative will be able to get inside Lydon's office and access the workstation without arousing suspicion. However, Lydon has a thirteen-year-old son, George, and a fifteen-year-old daughter, Sophie. It has been suggested that a pair of CHERUB agents may be able to befriend George and/or Sophie, infiltrate Kurt Lydon's home and then sabotage the centrifuge design.

6. INTRODUCING

'You boys OK?' John Jones asked, as he drove a Nissan 4x4 across a deserted roundabout. Andy and Greg sat in the back.

'All set, boss,' Greg nodded, before looking across at Andy. 'Just remember not to call me Rat.'

'OK, Rat,' Andy smirked.

John turned into a modern development of detached houses and slowed down so that he could catch the house numbers as he rolled by. At number twenty-two he turned on to a brick driveway and pulled up beside a silver Astra.

The boys reached over the back seat to grab their backpacks before following him up to the front door. A slim woman opened up before they had a chance to ring the bell. George hurried up the hallway behind her, dressed in a T-shirt and Futurama boxers.

'You must be Dr Lydon,' John smiled, giving himself a bit of an Australian accent so that he'd pass for Greg's dad. 'Thanks for having the boys. If there's any problem whatsoever just give me a call.'

'Call me Susie,' George's mum said, as she shook John's hand. 'It's no bother. They've got money for pizza and three dozen X-box games, so they'll pretty much take care of themselves.'

As the adults spoke on the doorstep, Greg and Andy ducked under Dr Lydon's arm, kicked off their trainers and headed upstairs to George's bedroom.

'You boys behave,' John shouted after them.

'No worries, Dad,' Greg shouted back. 'See you in the morning.'

The house was comfortable, but it wouldn't win any design awards and smelled slightly like cats. George had a smallish bedroom, but he had a cool AV setup with surround-sound speakers and a 37-inch LCD mounted on the wall. Zhang had arrived early and was playing *Forza Motorsport Two* with the volume turned up loud. He'd stripped down to a pair of Chelsea shorts because the room was stifling, and sat himself cross-legged on the end of George's bed.

'Nice bruises, Zhang,' Greg noted.

Zhang shook his head. 'It was nice of you to leave your Karate Kid act until *after* Johno battered me and stuck my head down the crapper.'

'Until today I thought getting your head stuck down the school toilet was just an urban myth,' Greg smiled, before looking across at Andy. 'This is my cousin. He's down from Scotland for the first week of the holiday.'

Zhang was driving a Dodge Challenger through a chicane, so he just made a grunting noise.

'You've got four controllers,' Andy smiled.

'Yeah,' George said proudly. 'You any good at *Virtua Tennis*? We can play a doubles tournament.'

'Bagsy not Zhang's team,' Greg blurted. 'He sucks.'

'Screw you,' Zhang shouted. 'You can't expect anyone to play brilliantly the first time you pick it up. I took you to a tiebreak that last set—

AAARGH, I hate that stupid corner *so* much!'

George cracked up laughing as Zhang's Challenger clattered through a gravel trap before smashing into a tyre wall.

'Tossers!' Zhang shouted, as he threw the controller at the bed. 'Second place – I had him all lined up to overtake on the next straight.'

The boys all jumped as George's mum's voice sounded in the doorway.

'Haven't you heard of knocking?' George tutted.

'I did knock,' she yelled. 'If you didn't have those speakers turned up so loud . . .'

George crawled across the floor and turned down the volume on his hi-fi.

'Sit up as long as you like and have your fun,' Dr Lydon said firmly. 'But I've been on at the hospital for sixteen hours and I'm going to bed as soon as I've had my shower, so keep the noise down. OK?'

'Don't worry, Mum,' George said. 'We'll be quieter than mice in silk slippers.'

George's mum smiled. 'There's crisps in the cupboard, Ben and Jerry's in the freezer and some of those microwave burrito thingies that you like. I'll leave you to it.'

Greg looked surprised as she headed down the corridor. 'So your mum's going to bed?'

George broke into a big smile. 'It's *so* mint!' he grinned. 'My dad's gone off for some business meeting in Belgium, Sophie's going out clubbing with one of her mates and my mum's just worked a double shift at the hospital. Once she's asleep we own this joint!'

'Cool,' Zhang said.

Andy and Greg exchanged covert smiles: the fewer people in the house, the easier it would be to access Kurt Lydon's computer.

'It gets better,' Greg said, as he pulled his sleeping bag off the top of his backpack and dragged out eight cans of beer.

George eyed them warily. 'If my mum sees that . . .'

Zhang tutted. 'Don't be a wuss, Georgie. It's only two cans each. It won't kill you.'

'Four each, actually,' Andy grinned. 'There's eight more in my bag.'

Zhang smiled at Andy. 'I'm starting to like you already, mate.'

'I suppose,' George said. 'But we'd better wait until my mum's asleep. And you'll have to take the empty cans home because if she sees that lot in the rubbish she'll kill me.'

'We're all getting hammered!' Zhang sang. 'We're all getting hammered.'

'Mind if I use your toilet, George?' Andy asked politely.

'Better than pissing on the carpet,' George smiled, as he opened his door and pointed along the hallway. 'Second door on the right.'

Across the hallway, George's sister Sophie stepped out of her room. She was dressed for a night out in black heels and a black dress that left plenty of flesh on display.

'Look boys,' George grinned. 'All done up like a dog's dinner.'

Sophie flicked her brother off. 'What's all this then?' she sneered. 'X-box and *Battlestar Galactica* DVDs? You're *such* a bunch of losers.'

'Yeah,' George scoffed. 'Much better to sit at the back of the cinema getting tongued by that chav Daniel.'

Sophie tutted with contempt as she headed down the hallway towards the bathroom, then banged furiously on the door when she realised that Andy was inside.

'Outta there, geeko!' she yelled.

'Use the one downstairs,' George said.

'I can't, thicko,' Sophie growled. 'Mum's in the shower.'

Andy was in a strange house with people he didn't know, so he apologised to Sophie as he emerged from the bathroom.

'Just get out my way,' she growled.

George shrugged apologetically as Andy headed back towards the bedroom.

'Sticks and stones,' Andy said casually.

'I know how to get her back,' George grinned, as he darted into his sister's room.

Seconds later, George emerged with a floppy-eared toy rabbit and plunged it headfirst down the front of his boxers.

'Oh you naughty rabbit!' George said noisily, as the other three boys burst out laughing.

George raced down the hall with the soft toy protruding ridiculously from his shorts and banged on the bathroom door.

'Sophie,' George said sweetly. 'Mr Rabbit's in trouble!'

'How many times?' Sophie shouted, as she burst

out of the bathroom with wet hands. 'Stay out of my room you little freak.'

But she didn't go really bananas until she saw the pair of furry legs sticking out of her brother's boxers.

'Dirty little git,' she screamed. 'You're getting such a slap.'

George started to run but Sophie wrapped an arm around her brother's waist as he scrambled through his bedroom doorway.

'Ooof,' Zhang laughed, as George took a brutal slap across the cheek. 'I felt that.'

Sophie ripped the bunny out of George's shorts before slapping his back and knocking him to the ground. 'Stay out of my room,' Sophie screamed. 'Don't you *ever* touch my stuff, geek.'

'You wait and see what I do while you're out,' George said, unperturbed by the huge red welt on his face. 'Mr Bunny has a date with my Stanley knife.'

Sophie pinned George against the hallway wall with her leg before bending forwards and grabbing his skinny ankles. There was a desperate turn in George's expression which the other lads didn't understand.

'Sophie, I'm sorry!' George gasped. 'Don't.'

George grasped at the door frame, but Sophie was way stronger than her scrawny brother and she started dragging him down the hallway. As she picked up speed, his bare back zipped across the shaggy nylon carpet.

'Noooo,' he screamed desperately. 'Mummmm!'

Greg, Andy and Zhang piled out into the corridor to watch. As George sat up, his three friends saw the bright red friction burn caused by his high speed ride across the carpet. George screwed up his face in pain, but didn't want his mates to see that he was hurting.

'Stay out of my room, loser,' Sophie shouted.

'Evil bitch,' George shouted back.

Downstairs a door clicked open and George's mum stormed out of the shower room in a pastel green dressing gown and matching slippers.

'Pack it in,' she shouted. 'I'm *so* sick of you two. You're thirteen and fifteen, but you act like you're still three and five. Look what you've done to his back!'

'Oh, why not take his side for a change, Mum?' Sophie said sarcastically. 'He stuck Mr Rabbit's head down his pissy shorts. All I want is for the little prick to stay out of my room.'

'Why can't you just die of cancer?' George shouted, as he grabbed the banister and hauled himself up.

Sophie poked out her tongue. 'Loser,' she hissed.

George's mum growled furiously. 'How many times have I told you to stay out of each other's rooms?'

'I can't trust him,' Sophie shouted. 'I'm gonna come home and find pizza crusts in my bed or something.'

'Just get out of my sight, Sophie,' her mum shouted. 'Your father put locks on all the doors to stop this nonsense. Have you turned the key?'

'I can't find it,' Sophie admitted.

George's mum pointed her daughter downstairs at the front door. 'I've got a spare. Now get out of this house before I really lose my temper and ground the pair of you.'

As Sophie slammed the front door, her mum steamed down the hallway towards the other three boys, who'd all disappeared into George's room because she looked like she'd bite the head off anyone who dared open their mouth.

She leaned into Sophie's room and spotted the supposedly lost key amidst the jumble of hair products and GCSE revision on the desk.

'Right,' George's mum said, as she locked Sophie's room and put the key in her dressing-gown pocket. 'You boys might be on holidays, but I've got to go to work tomorrow. So have fun, but if anyone wakes me up there's gonna be major eruptions.'

7. TREES

George slowly closed the door of his mum's bedroom, feeling a little woozy as he crept down the hallway towards his room. It was almost ten and nearly dark outside, but it was still boiling hot, so the four boys just wore shorts.

'She's soundo,' George grinned as he stepped back into his room.

The room smelled mostly like pizza, but there was also a whiff of beer and sweat. The floor was strewn with crumbs and pizza boxes, while Zhang had added to the carnage by stepping up on George's bed and sticking a slice of cheese-topped garlic bread to the ceiling.

'More beer?' Greg asked, as he pulled out a can.

'Don't mind if I do,' Zhang slurred.

Before handing the beer across, Greg tilted the can, making sure there was a little blue mark on the bottom: they'd brought sixteen identical looking cans, but the contents had been tampered with by the technical team on CHERUB campus.

The ones with blue marks were for George and Zhang and contained full strength beer, injected with a powerful sedative. The beer in the unmarked cans had been sucked out and replaced with an alcohol-free variety. If the plan worked out, George and Zhang would get drunk and crash out, while CHERUB agents Greg and Andy remained wide awake and sober.

'Check this out, babes,' George shouted jubilantly as he threw his bedroom window wide open and climbed up on to the ledge.

Andy and Greg were horrified as George hurled himself through the first-floor window. They were supposed to be monitoring how drunk George and Zhang got and their mission would go straight down the toilet if someone ended up in casualty.

There was a crunch of branches followed by a triumphant whoop from George as Andy and Greg leaned out of the window. George was laughing wildly as he clambered out of a dense hedge.

'I've *always* wanted to try that,' George said, as he collapsed backwards on to the lawn, howling with laughter and thumping his chest. 'Much beer give caveman George courage.'

Despite his initial alarm, Greg realised that the hedge was huge and the drop on to it from the first-floor window less than two metres.

'Come on you pussies,' George shouted. 'It's such a rush.'

Andy pointed to the strapping around his chest. 'I don't want to rip this lot off.'

Greg had no such qualms and vaulted on to the window ledge before diving face first into the huge hedge. The leaves and branches were prickly, but it was a riot having the thick shrubbery crashing around his head and then trying to untangle himself.

Greg had only drunk alcohol-free beer, but he had to act drunk so he howled like a loon as he staggered out on to the lawn. Zhang seemed less confident as he climbed on to the window ledge.

'Come on down, fat-boy,' George taunted.

George and Greg cheered as Zhang crashed forward out of the window. At first it looked the same as when the first two boys dropped, but Zhang's weight pushed him deeper into the hedge and there was an almighty snap of wood as one of the main stems holding up the hedge snapped.

'AAAARGH!' Zhang screamed.

He ended up with his legs high in the air, atop a giant clump of snapped hedge strewn across the back lawn.

Zhang wasn't hurt and Greg laughed as he helped him up, but George was freaking out over the state of the hedge.

'My dad's gonna slaughter me,' George gasped.

Greg grabbed the main chunk of the broken hedge and rested it against the intact pieces on either side. 'Good as new,' he grinned.

'It's not funny you guys!' George moaned, as he crouched over and picked up leaves and snapped branches scattered over the lawn.

A torch flickered on in the garden next door and an old woman's voice came from behind the fence. 'What the devil's going on out there?'

'Miss Hampstead,' George gasped, as he started

running around the side of the house.

'Go back indoors, you nosy old bat,' Zhang shouted.

'She's Sophie's godmother: practically family,' George whispered. He gave Zhang a shove before looking up towards his bedroom window. 'Andy, get downstairs and open the front door before she shines that light over the fence!'

Andy smiled thoughtfully out of the window. 'I might do,' he grinned.

Andy laughed as the other three scrambled up the driveway, yelping as chunks of gravel dug into their bare feet. When they got inside George looked up the stairs nervously, half expecting the racket to have woken his mum up.

The boys muffled their giggles as they headed up the stairs, but Zhang held his hand over his mouth to stifle a huge yawn.

'Man, I'm knackered all of a sudden,' Zhang complained, stepping back into George's bedroom and crashing backwards on to the bed.

'Know what you mean,' George nodded, as he caught the yawn. 'That beer's given me a headache.'

'Can't take your drink,' Greg teased, as he looked

at his watch and saw that it was ten-fifteen. It was ninety minutes since George and Zhang had taken their first mouthful of drugged beer and the sedative was kicking in right on schedule.

'We never got around to *Virtua Tennis*,' Andy said, as George slumped on to a leather beanbag. 'You guys up for it?'

Zhang had his eyes closed and George waved his hand in front of his face. 'You start off, I need a few minutes' rest.'

Greg loaded the tennis game into the X-box and turned the hi-fi volume down low as he grabbed one of the wireless controllers. The two CHERUB agents played half-heartedly. Andy won the first set on a tiebreak, but there were no protests or celebrations.

Instead, Andy leaned across the bed and pinched Zhang's cheek, while Greg crept across the carpet and jabbed George's thigh with his big toe.

'Sleeping like babies,' Greg said. 'Get the kit.'

Andy unzipped a pocket on the side of his backpack and pulled out a plastic wallet. It looked like a packet of felt-tips, but instead of pens it contained twelve identical syringes filled with a fast-acting sedative. The sedative in the beer worked for less than two hours and it was hard to tell exactly how much they'd drunk. George and Zhang had to be injected with something more powerful to ensure that they didn't wake up.

Even the gentlest of injections can turn into a small swelling and a bruise which looks obvious on open skin, so Andy had to inject an area of the body that's hard to inspect.

'Show me some butt,' Andy grinned.

Greg rolled Zhang on to his belly and pulled down the back of his boxers.

'Gross,' Greg choked, gagging and turning away. 'It's skidmark city down there.'

Andy tried not to breathe as he pulled Zhang's buttock upwards and wiped a patch of skin with a sterile wipe. He then dug the needle into the fold where Zhang's flabby bum met the back of his thigh.

After injecting enough sedative to keep Zhang under for six hours, Greg hitched up the boxers and rolled Zhang on to his back again. George weighed half as much and showered twice as often, so it was a much more pleasant experience rolling him off the beanbag and injecting his buttock as he lay flat on the floor.

Greg tucked a pillow under George's head before looking uneasily towards Andy. 'Two down, one to go.'

'The tricky one,' Andy noted, as he pulled a green cylinder and a gas mask out of his backpack before heading down the hallway behind Greg.

Dr Lydon was probably asleep, but she wasn't sedated like the boys and would wake with a start before they got anywhere near sticking a needle in her butt. She had to be taken down in a two-stage process, the first of which involved a powerful knock-out gas.

Greg approached first, quietly opening the bedroom door and stepping into the gloomy room. If Dr Lydon had been awake, he'd have pretended to have walked into the wrong room on the way to the toilet, but the doctor was dead to the world after her double shift at the hospital.

'Clear,' Greg said, as he backed out.

Andy tightened the straps of the gas mask behind his head and leaned into the room holding the pressurised cylinder. He pointed the nozzle up at the ceiling over the double bed and pressed the trigger to release a gentle mist. Job done, Andy backed out and swiftly pulled shut the door.

'Give it four minutes for the gas to clear out of the air,' Greg said, looking at his watch as Andy pulled off his mask and tucked it back inside his pack, along with the gas cylinder.

After an anxious wait crouching in the hallway, Andy burst noisily into Dr Lydon's bedroom. He flicked on the light and stumbled on to the bed. This was a deliberate strategy: if the gas hadn't worked for some reason, he'd get yelled at for waking George's mum but she'd hopefully think nothing of it apart from some hyped-up kid bursting through the wrong door.

In many ways this was the trickiest part of the whole operation, so Andy was delighted to find himself sprawled over Dr Lydon's legs, with the mattress bouncing but the doctor's body completely limp.

'Gimme a needle,' Andy shouted, as he ripped off the duvet.

The boys were slightly freaked out as the bedding landed on the floor. They'd both been through

CHERUB training and were capable of all sorts of remarkable feats, but it was still a shock seeing one of your mate's mums sprawled naked and unconscious over the bed in front of you.

'I feel like a right perv,' Greg confessed, as he rolled Dr Lydon on to her front.

'Snap some pics with your camera phone,' Andy grinned. 'That'll freak Georgie boy out when he wakes up.'

'Be serious,' Greg said, snorting with laughter as he swabbed Dr Lydon's skin with a sterile wipe before Andy plunged the needle into the back of her thigh.

Greg threw the duvet back over the doctor before following Andy out into the hallway. He'd flipped his phone open to dial their mission controller.

'John,' Andy said cheerfully. 'Phase one's in the bag. Everyone's sedated and we're about to move into Kurt Lydon's study.'

8. WINDOWS

Kurt Lydon's study was locked, but that's not a major problem for a CHERUB agent. Greg opened the door easily, using a straight pick attached to his lock gun. Two bedrooms had been knocked together to create Kurt's workspace and thirty thousand pounds had been invested in specialised computer equipment.

Two powerful Dell workstations hummed away inside a special cooling cabinet and there was a huge inkjet plotter for making blueprints. One wall shelved thick books with titles like *Advanced Molecular Thermodynamics* and *Mathematical Modelling for Turbulent Plumes and Jets*. Pride of place went to a pair of 30-inch ultra-high-resolution

LCD panels, worth over ten grand apiece. Beside Kurt's regular keyboard and mouse was a multi-buttoned spaceball controller, designed for manipulating 3D images on screen.

Andy had spent hours practising with an identical system on CHERUB campus, but still felt intimidated as he sank into Kurt Lydon's high-backed office chair. He tapped the space bar and was pleased to see that the computer was only in standby, but the screen demanded a password.

Greg was already on the case. He'd sneaked into the room on an after-school visit two weeks earlier and installed a hardware keylogger between the keyboard plug and the USB port on the back of Kurt's main computer.

Keyloggers contain memory chips that record every keystroke entered into a computer. When the logger got back to the MI5 lab it would hopefully reveal all sorts of information that Kurt had typed over the previous fortnight, but all they needed right now was Kurt's main password.

Greg pulled a tiny laptop out of his backpack, plugged in the keylogger and sat on the floor while the machine booted up.

'We haven't got all night,' Andy moaned.

'Keep your wig on,' Greg teased. 'These tiny laptops aren't very powerful. It takes a couple of minutes to boot up and there's diddly squat I can do about it.'

Andy hated waiting around. Missions were OK when his mind was occupied, but he had a nervous disposition and waiting always made him start thinking about stuff that could go wrong.

'OK,' Greg said when he'd finally accessed the keylogger data. 'First session, last Friday week. Capital A R then lower case *i s t o t l e* followed by a hash, a percentage sign and the numbers five, three, one and eight.'

Andy was relieved that Windows accepted the password. 'Never would have guessed that one,' he gasped, as the desktop and taskbar appeared on screen.

The screen was specifically designed for high resolution work, which left the dozens of tiny icons looking like specks amidst the huge expanse of screen. Greg put his laptop on the carpet and passed Andy a ring-binder and CD-rom from his backpack.

Andy placed the silver disc in a tray and let the Dell swallow it. A dialogue box popped up on screen and he clicked OK to install a forensic program designed by the security services, known as Window Breaker. The program froze time, ensuring that no time and date stamps were left when files were altered. It also enabled a back door into the Windows operating system that bypassed most Windows security protocols.

The second program on the CD was a Trojan horse. Once installed, MI5 would be able to access Kurt's computer, remotely reading his files and monitoring all activity. The instant the program was installed, Kurt's anti-virus software flashed up a warning. Andy had fully expected this and the third program on the CD dealt with it by installing a patch that made the anti-virus turn a blind eye to the unwanted software.

'OK, that's the software installed,' Andy smiled. 'You'd better start hunting for the dreaded backups.'

Andy planned to spend most of the next three hours altering Kurt's centrifuge design so that it wouldn't work. Greg had to search the office and the rest of the house and overwrite any backup copies he could find with a doctored version of the original stolen file.

But this left MI5 with two major headaches. First, if Kurt looked back at any previous versions of his work for any reason he'd realise that the files had been tampered with. Second, there was no way of knowing whether Kurt had stashed an extra backup under the floorboards, at a friend's house, or even in a safety deposit box on the other side of town.

All MI5 could do about this was cross their fingers, not let Lydon out of sight and move swiftly to arrest him if he began to suspect that he was under surveillance.

'Remember,' Andy said, 'it's a twenty-gigabyte file, so it won't fit on a memory stick or a DVD. You're only looking for backup hard drives.'

Greg sounded slightly irritated. 'I know, Andy. I read the briefing too.'

He started off by running a search on the hard drives of Kurt Lydon's twin servers as Andy opened Lydon's AutoCAD software and found the latest version of the centrifuge design. The 3D model comprised over three thousand parts and even on one of the fastest PCs available it took nearly two minutes to load.

Once Andy was sure that he'd opened the right file he plugged a portable hard drive into the USB port on the front of the machine and made a duplicate copy. MI5 would study this file to establish how quickly Kurt was progressing with his simplified design.

By the time this was finished, Greg had overwritten a file on the other PC and began searching drawers and shelves for backup drives.

Andy now had to enter the alterations that would sabotage Kurt's redesign work. A hundred and forty-three parts had to be changed, and each one required up to a dozen individual alterations.

It was impossible to remember all of these, so one of Lydon's former colleagues had made a checklist, complete with detailed instructions, screenshots and even printouts of specific menus within the sophisticated software. It was delicate work: one decimal point in the wrong place could leave an obvious flaw in the design that would make Kurt

Lydon suspicious and blow the whole operation.

Andy put one hand over the spaceball and another over the keyboard before muttering 'Concentrate,' to himself.

He opened the ring-binder and started to read: *Alteration one, locate part spacer bearing seventeen.* Andy navigated expertly with the spaceball, finding the part using the search tool, zooming in and then changing the display properties so that the wire frame outline of his target part was the only thing on screen.

Select the fourth and sixth sprocket holes. Alter the thread properties from one sixteenth of a millimetre to one eighteenth of a millimetre. Rotate the object in relationship to the Y-axis within the main design by point zero seven of a degree.

It was brain numbing stuff and it wasn't helped by Greg humming as he rifled noisily through a filing cabinet.

'Dude,' Andy said fiercely. 'Shut up.'

Greg didn't appreciate the tone, but he'd seen the complexity of Andy's instructions and didn't envy his task. 'Sorry mate,' he said. 'I'll be done searching here in a minute anyway.'

Two hours later, Andy sat at the giant screens rubbing tired eyes. Greg took a mouthful of Pepsi and popped a couple of M&Ms in his mouth. Greg had inspected the family PC and George's laptop, but the only centrifuge design he'd found was an original stored on a backup hard drive on top of a kitchen cabinet.

To speed Andy's task, Greg now stood alongside with the ring-binder, reading his instructions out loud. The operation wasn't going badly and they were ahead of schedule, but the task required absolute concentration and it was three hours past when they'd normally be in bed.

'Alteration one hundred,' Greg said, sounding slightly triumphant because they'd finally progressed to a three-digit number. 'Open the sub-model of the motor unit G and alter the specification of the insulation . . .'

Greg didn't finish because his phone started to vibrate. It was their mission controller.

'How's it going?' John asked.

'Not too shabby,' Greg said. 'It doesn't look like Kurt's too thorough about backing up his data and we should be finished inside an hour if we're not interrupted.'

'Out of luck on that score, I'm afraid,' John said. 'They're triangulating the position of Sophie Lydon's mobile phone in the control room on campus. She called for a cab a while back and it looks like she'll be home in six to eight minutes.'

Greg glanced at his watch and saw that it was only half-past one. 'Didn't you tell me that the club was open till three?'

'It might well be,' John said. 'But you don't *have* to stay till closing time. Don't get discouraged, you've got all the equipment and we made plans for an interruption. Wait until Sophie goes to sleep, then use the gas and the needle, like with her mother.'

'I know the plan,' Greg said reluctantly, before tapping Andy on the shoulder. 'We'd better clear out.'

'Bloody Sophie,' Andy complained, as Greg snapped his phone shut. 'Would have been so much simpler if she'd waited till we were done.'

The two boys stuck all their stuff back inside their packs, hurried back into George's bedroom and threw their sleeping bags out on the floor.

Andy was tense, but he couldn't help but see the funny side of Zhang's loud snoring.

It was less than ten minutes, but it felt like ages before Sophie's key rattled in the front door. She hurried down the hallway and used the downstairs toilet, before staggering upstairs, barefoot, with a bottle of Highland Spring water in one hand and her black heels hanging from the other.

Andy peeked out of the open doorway and saw that Sophie was drunk. Her head bopped to a tune in her mind and she was murmuring the line of a song to herself, over and over.

Instead of heading into her own room, Sophie ratcheted up the tension by poking her head inside George's open door. Greg and Andy closed their eyes and kept dead still.

'Ahh, the little geeks are sleeping,' she muttered to herself, before giggling.

Sophie started to back out, but noticed Andy's bag of M&Ms and a half-drunk can of beer on the carpet.

'Mummy won't be happy if she sees that, little brother,' Sophie grinned, before tilting the can to take a swig.

Andy and Greg weren't sure if the can was drugged or alcohol-free, but it didn't really matter because they needed to get on with the operation and couldn't wait two hours to put Sophie to sleep.

The beer was warm and flat, so Sophie spat it out in disgust. Greg opened one eye slightly, and saw Sophie's painted toenails on the carpet just a few centimetres away from his face.

'I'll teach you to mess with Mr Rabbit,' Sophie slurred.

Smiling mischievously, she poured Andy's M&Ms on to the carpet near the doorway and then crunched them under her heel. Once they were nicely mashed she tipped the remainder of the beer on to the brightly-coloured mess. Even if the liquid dried up by morning, a multicoloured stain and the distinctive smell of beer would remain.

'Talk your way out of that one, Georgie boy,' Sophie said quietly.

She gave her bum a jubilant wiggle and laughed drunkenly as she staggered out and grabbed the handle of her bedroom door, but it was still locked from earlier.

Greg and Andy realised the same thing at the same time: George's mum had hidden the key so that the boys couldn't get back into Sophie's room. The only way Sophie could get into her room would be to ask her mum where the key was and if Sophie went into her mum's room and found that she wouldn't wake up she'd scream the house down.

9. PLANS

There was a lot at stake: a corrupt scientist, a centrifuge design worth millions, the chance to infiltrate the highest levels of the Dark Sun network and the opportunity to stop some crazed dictator or terrorist getting their hands on a nuclear bomb a few years down the line.

Greg and Andy hoped some scenario from their training would leap out with a solution, but all they felt was blind panic as Sophie headed drunkenly down the hallway towards her mother's bedroom.

'Try unlocking her door,' Greg whispered to Andy, as he darted out into the hallway. 'Hey Sophie. What's up?'

Sophie put a hand on her hip and looked at Greg as if he was something nasty on the bottom of her shoe. 'Piss off back to bed,' she tutted.

'I saw what you just did with the M&Ms,' Greg warned. 'I had one eye open the whole time.'

Sophie shrugged. 'My mum's never gonna believe you.'

'She might,' Greg said, as he stopped walking half a metre from Sophie. He didn't have a clue what to say, so he blurted the first thing that came into his head. 'I might forget all about it if you give us a quick snog.'

Sophie tutted incredulously. 'In your dreams, pervert.'

'Come on,' Greg said. He was about the same height as Sophie and he put his hand on her shoulder. 'Just a quick Frenchie.'

'EUGHH!' Sophie shuddered, before giving Greg a two-handed push. 'Touch me again and I'll knock your block off.'

Down the hallway, Andy turned his body so that Sophie couldn't see what he was up to as he worked on her door with the lock gun. Sophie felt intimidated as she backed up towards the chest near the staircase: Greg was only twelve, but he looked strong and she knew that he'd seen off two Year Ten boys.

Greg sensed Sophie's fear and took a step back. 'I'm only messing,' he said. 'I'm not gonna hurt you.'

'Ta-da!' Andy said, from down the hallway, throwing the lock gun back into George's room as he pushed Sophie's door open.

'Sorted,' Greg smiled, as he looked down the hallway. 'Now you don't need to wake your mum up.'

But the booze in Sophie's bloodstream made her paranoid and Greg's attempt at blackmail, followed by a sudden eagerness to please, was totally creeping her out. The instant Greg turned to look back at Andy, she grabbed a vase off the cabinet at the top of the stairs.

Greg saw it move out the corner of his eye, but Sophie was fast and brought the vase down hard over the back of his head. It didn't break over his skull, but slipped from Sophie's grasp and shattered on the wooden acorn at the top of the stair rail.

'Keep your hands off me, weirdo,' Sophie screamed, as she followed up with a remarkably well-aimed Karate kick.

Even two years of the best combat training can't protect you when you're taken by surprise. Greg doubled over and groaned with pain as Sophie stormed down the hallway towards Andy.

'Where's the key?' Sophie demanded. 'I swear, if you guys have touched *anything* inside my room . . .'

'There's no key,' Andy said. 'I just know how to pick locks.'

'You're so full of it,' Sophie screamed. She felt confident after flattening Greg and gave Andy an almighty shove.

'Gimme my key,' Sophie shouted, as she launched a full fledged assault by trying to knee Andy in the stomach.

Unlike Greg, Andy saw it coming. He sidestepped Sophie's flying knee, which was a good job because she was hefty and it hit the passage wall so hard that it made a dent in the plasterboard.

As Sophie groaned and clutched her agonised knee, Andy hooked his foot around Sophie's standing leg and swept it from under her. Andy stepped back, leaving Sophie glowering up at him from the floor.

'I was trying to help,' Andy said, trying to calm her down. 'Why don't you just go to bed, eh?'

But Sophie was having none of it and she lunged forward and tried wrapping her arms around Andy's waist. Meantime, Greg was back on his feet. He felt an excruciating pain as he took his first step, but he ignored it as he sprinted down the hallway and dived into George's bedroom.

Sophie was much heavier than Andy, but her Karate skills were limited to a few self-defence classes and Andy soon straddled her waist, pinning her arms to her side.

'Please calm down,' Andy said. 'You're drunk. You'll feel better if you get in bed and try going to sleep.'

'I want that key,' she screamed. 'I don't want you little idiots in my room.'

Greg burrowed down the side pocket of Andy's pack and grabbed one of the syringes. Out in the hall, Sophie spat and wriggled, even though Andy had her hopelessly pinned.

'Get off me,' she yelled.

'As soon as you calm down,' Andy yelled back. 'It's a misunderstanding. I haven't got any key, I swear.'

Greg crouched down behind Andy. He put the syringe between his teeth, before grabbing Sophie's foot and twisting it around so that it was flat to the floor.

'I'll kill you both,' Sophie screamed, now close to tears. 'Lemme go.'

Andy felt bad because Sophie was really upset, but she was going so crazy that he knew he'd only have to pin her again if he let her up.

Greg took the needle and jabbed it into the flesh between two toes on Sophie's right foot. She felt something, but Andy's torso blocked her view so she had no idea what it was.

It took half a minute for the sedative to start working. Sophie stopped thrashing about and her body started to relax.

'Thank Christ for that,' Andy gasped breathlessly, as he tried to stand up.

But the mixture of nightclub cocktails, panic and sedative hadn't done Sophie any good. As Andy lifted his weight off her stomach, she sat upright and spewed bright green vomit into his lap.

'Ahh shit!' Andy gasped, heaving at the smell of the puke dripping off his thighs as Sophie crashed back on to the carpet, dead to the world.

It's easy to choke when you're unconscious and Andy's first-aid training kicked in. He plunged his hand into Sophie's mouth and made sure that her airway was clear, before standing up and rolling her into the recovery position.

'Who'd want to be a spy?' Andy complained, clutching the strained muscles down his left side as he stepped back from Sophie. 'How come you never see James Bond covered in some drunk bird's puke?'

Greg wasn't listening because he had his own problems. He leaned against the wall, inspecting his right heel. He'd ignored the pain when the adrenalin was flowing, but now realised that he'd sliced his foot open on a chunk of the broken vase. What's more, he'd left a trail of blood all along the hallway carpet and into George's room too.

Andy inspected the mess: blood, puke, beer, broken china, half a bag of crushed M&Ms and even a dent in the wall. 'George's old lady's gonna love this when she wakes up in the morning.'

Andy and Greg were both in pain, but they'd been through worse in CHERUB training and were both determined to pull off their mission.

Greg looked up and smiled at Andy, then mimicked the gruff voice of a CHERUB instructor. 'This is tough but cherubs are tougher,' he said.

Andy laughed, but that made the torn muscles in his stomach hurt even more.

'I'll take a shower and nick a clean pair of shorts from George's wardrobe,' he said. 'You find a bandage or something to stop your foot from bleeding. Once we're cleaned up, we'll drag Sophie on to her bed.'

'Fair enough,' Greg nodded. 'Then what?'

Andy glanced at his watch. 'It's only one forty-five. Nobody will be waking up for at least three hours, so we go back into Kurt's study, make the last forty-three revisions to the centrifuge design and then turn in for whatever's left of the night.'

'Sounds like a plan to me,' Greg nodded, as he started hobbling towards the bathroom.

10. RAGE

Earthquakes are measured on the Richter scale, tornados on the Fujita scale, and there's an Explosivity Index for volcanoes. Andy and Greg weren't sure what scale was used for enraged mothers, but whatever it was George's mum hit the top level when she woke up at half-past seven that Saturday morning.

'Get your arses downstairs,' Dr Lydon screamed, as she yanked George out of a gentle slumber. Being gassed had left her with a bad headache, which made her mood even worse. 'Mind your feet, there's broken china all along the passageway.'

She'd seen the carnage in the hallway, but only learned of the busted hedge when she threw open George's window to clear out the smell of beer and pizza.

'No more sleepovers, ever,' she screamed. 'This is *way* beyond a joke.'

Apart from the hedge, everything had been fine when George and Zhang dropped off to sleep. George was stunned when he saw the state of the hallway.

'It wasn't me!' he protested meekly.

Across the hall, Sophie emerged with her hair pointing in a thousand different directions, still dressed in her black dress and stockings, but now accessorised with dried-out vomit. 'What's all the noise?' she moaned. 'I need sleep.'

'Sleep,' Dr Lydon screamed, as George and Zhang scrambled down the stairs in a state of complete panic. 'Young lady, nobody in this house is getting sleep until every speck of this mess is cleaned up.'

Sophie tutted. 'Don't blow your stack, Ma. It's not my fault if the geekboys decided to get drunk.'

'That was you!' George's mum shouted, pointing at the puke on the carpet. 'It's all down your dress. Get down to the kitchen and grab the cleaning stuff from under the sink.'

'You're so sexist, just because I'm a girl.'

'Oh don't you worry,' Dr Lydon hissed. 'George is doing his share of the cleaning too, and you're both paying for the damage out of pocket money and birthday money. And that includes new carpets if we need 'em, so you'd better scrub hard.'

Down in the kitchen Zhang was helping himself to Coco Pops and seemed to find the whole scenario quite amusing. 'Pity you're not coming to China with me, Georgie,' Zhang laughed. 'It's about the only place you'd be safe from that crazed mother of yours.'

George was less concerned with Zhang's teasing than with the breach of trust by his new friend Greg.

'I've had loads of sleepovers before, and nothing like this has ever happened,' George yelled. 'What the hell were you guys playing at?'

Greg tried to act innocent. 'Your sister came home drunk and couldn't get into her room. Andy knows how to pick locks so he tried to help, but Sophie went psycho when we opened her door.'

George wasn't sure he believed this. 'What about

the massive stain on my carpet? That must have been you guys, and why's Andy wearing a pair of my shorts?'

'Because your dumb-ass sister threw up all over me and then passed out,' Andy said.

At this point Sophie came storming in and started grabbing sponges, cloths and a bottle of carpet shampoo from under the sink. 'You're helping, George,' she steamed. 'None of this would have happened if it wasn't for your idiot mates.'

'You were drunk,' Greg shouted. 'You went crazy. You smashed a vase over my head.'

'Because you groped me,' Sophie shouted back.

'I didn't grope you! And we saw you rubbing beer and M&Ms into George's carpet to get him into trouble.'

'That's such a lie,' Sophie shrieked.

Greg knew he had her. 'Then why's the bottom of your foot all green and red?'

Sophie didn't move, but George closed in and demanded to look.

'Show me,' George yelled.

Sophie refused to lift her foot and when George tried to make her she smacked him around the back of the head. George immediately sank his teeth into his sister's arm and two seconds later the two siblings were rolling around on the floor between the washing machine and the dining table, beating the living daylights out of each other.

'STOP IT,' George's mum screamed, dragging Sophie off her brother as she stormed into the kitchen. 'I'm not joking! You're both cleaning that mess up.'

Sophie huffed and grabbed the cleaning stuff off the floor, but George tried a different tack and burst into tears.

'I'm sorry,' George howled. 'Please don't punish us. Please don't ruin the whole summer holidays.'

Dr Lydon was having none of that. 'You're thirteen years old,' she sneered. 'Act like it. You think I'm gonna fall for that little act?'

To emphasise her point Dr Lydon grabbed a plastic dustpan out of the cupboard and whacked her son across the back of the legs.

'Get upstairs and start helping your sister,' she roared.

It was only about the third time Dr Lydon had ever hit one of her kids and George was so stunned that he bolted upstairs like someone had shoved a rocket up his butt.

With her own kids out of the way, Dr Lydon turned and scowled at Greg, Andy and Zhang, who all sat around the dining table. She was still holding the dustpan and clearly would have been happy to smack the pores off their faces. Unfortunately for her, parents are only allowed to be horrible to their own kids.

'Call your parents,' the doctor growled. 'I want you three out of my house – and don't ever expect to come back.'

George's mum then turned on her heel and steamed up the staircase. 'I don't hear any scrubbing up there,' she shouted.

Once she was out of earshot, Zhang rattled the cereal box on the table. 'Anyone for Coco Pops?' he asked cheerfully, as Andy pulled out his mobile to call John.

'My uncle's gonna meet us at the bottom of the road in ten minutes,' Andy said, when the call finished. 'We might as well go now, before the dragon lady comes back downstairs.'

'Damned good sleepover if you ask me,' Zhang

smirked, as he topped up his bowl. 'Normally I just kick George's butt on the X-box until I get bored, then I hold him down and fart on his head. But having you guys here, trashing the house and everything, has made a real nice change.'

'Maybe we'll go to your house next time,' Greg smiled, as he stretched his fist across the table and touched Zhang knuckle to knuckle.

'Nice meeting you, Zhang,' Andy said, as he did the same. 'Have a good month in China.'

The two CHERUB agents grabbed their packs and headed out of the back doorway. Andy was hurting all down his left side and Greg limped on his cut foot as they walked down the gravel driveway and turned on to the street.

'I've got a massive egg on my head where Sophie hit me with the vase,' Greg complained.

'We're like a couple of old men,' Andy said. 'But at least I can go back to calling you Rat now. This whole Greg thing is confusing.'

Greg had grown fond of Zhang and George and felt a touch sad. Now the mission was completed, CHERUB would invent some excuse why he had to move away and he'd never see either of them again. On the upside, Greg hadn't been near his girlfriend Lauren in two months and there'd be a mad party on campus when he turned thirteen in a couple of weeks' time.

'Feel sorry for old George,' Andy noted. 'It wasn't deliberate, but we totally stitched the poor guy up.'

'He'll survive,' Greg laughed. 'We got the job done and that's what counts.'

EPILOGUE

March 6th 2008 – World Book Day
The grass was stiff with frost, but the kids walking across CHERUB campus were happy because they'd all been allowed out of lessons to attend the opening ceremony for a new building. The two-storey structure was an eco-friendly design, with straw-insulated walls and a dramatic, curved, glass frontage.

The little red-shirt kids showed their enthusiasm by running in circles outside the main entrance, jumping up and down and generally going nuts. Older kids were more reserved, hanging back with their mates and trying not to show any enthusiasm in case it didn't look cool.

Lauren Adams led one of the biggest groups. Her boyfriend Rat (AKA Greg) walked alongside with his arm around her back while Andy walked with Lauren's best friend Bethany. Lauren's older brother James was behind with his best friend Bruce and a couple of his other mates bringing up the rear.

'It's freezing,' Chairwoman Zara Asker said, once the crowd around the new building had settled. 'So I'm gonna keep my speech short. We have a lot of special facilities on CHERUB campus, but our previous library was demolished to make way for the new mission control building. Today is World Book Day, so it gives me extra delight to officially declare the new CHERUB campus library open for business!'

There was a gentle bout of clapping as two of the smallest red-shirts walked up to a ribbon stretched across the main door, each holding one side of a pair of giant scissors. The crowd laughed as the ribbon refused to cut until it was held tight by two members of staff.

With more than two hundred people filtering through the doors, it was several minutes before

Lauren and her friends made it inside.

'Pretty swish,' Lauren said, as she looked up at the library's high-tech curved-oak ceiling and wavy glass frontage. There were desks and reference books on a gantry up above. At the far end was a refuge for little kids, filled with cushions and beanbags, in the middle of which was a five-metre-long pirate ship complete with a line of reading hammocks, an antique ship's wheel and white sails with the CHERUB logo printed on them.

The opposite end was designed for older kids, with armchairs, sofas and tables. An espresso machine provided coffee or frothy hot chocolate and there were baskets of muffins, croissants and fruit. Signs on the wall above the food said: *Please take a free drink and eat our freshly-baked muffins while you read. We can also offer fifty punishment laps to anyone who takes food or drink into the main library!*

Because of the sheer numbers of people, Lauren's group had to fight its way through just to get near the lounge area.

'It looks pretty swanky,' James Adams said, as he stared at the ceiling. 'But I've never really seen the point of books. I mean, if they're any good you just have to wait a couple of years and it gets turned into a movie.'

Lauren tutted. 'Just because the last book you read was about a hippo learning to tell the time.'

'And he never finished that,' Rat giggled. 'James still gets the big hand and the little hand mixed up.'

By this time, Lauren had reached the edge of the lounge area, but there was a horrendous queue to use the coffee machine, all the seats were taken and there were even kids perching on the coffee tables.

'It's only 'cos it's new,' Lauren's best friend Bethany noted. 'Come back in two days and there'll be four people in here.'

'It's really nice though,' Andy said thoughtfully. 'I mean, I'd rather sit here and read or do my homework than be alone in my room, and it looks like they've spent a bundle on new books.'

There was a loud crack and a couple of screams at the other end of the room. Everyone looked around and saw one of the masts snapping on the pirate ship.

'Timber!' James shouted.

'Well,' Lauren sighed. 'Whoever designed that clearly underestimated the destructive power of two dozen sugar-fuelled red-shirts.'

While chaos ensued at the opposite end, with staff rushing in to untangle yelling red-shirts from the sails on the broken mast, James spotted an empty table in the main part of the library and pointed towards it. 'We're never gonna get in the lounge. Let's go sit over there.'

James and Lauren led the way, but Rat stopped following when he spotted a familiar face on the front of a newspaper.

'Andy, check this out,' Rat yelled, as he held up the picture on the front page. 'Kurt Lydon.'

Andy came rushing over as Rat started reading the article:

BRITISH SCIENTIST AMONG TWENTY-TWO ARRESTED IN SWOOP ON NUKE TRAFFICKING NETWORK

A British nuclear engineer was one of twenty-two suspects arrested in Brussels at what police describe as the annual conference of a secretive nuclear trafficking network known as Dark Sun.

Fifty-four-year-old Kurt Lydon from Milton Keynes is a uranium enrichment expert who specialises in the design of gas centrifuges used to make fuel for atomic weapons.

The joint operation was organised by British, French, American and Belgian intelligence services and follows the explosion at a prototype uranium enrichment facility in a remote area of Nigeria three weeks ago.

Lydon is thought to have been the mastermind behind the design of the Nigerian centrifuge. Despite the explosion, which was initially picked up by radiological monitoring equipment on board an American spy satellite, Nigerian authorities continue to distance themselves from the explosion and have described Dark Sun as a 'terrorist organisation with no connection to the democratically-elected government of Nigeria'.

An MI5 press officer described last night's arrests in Belgium as a 'colossal blow' to those countries who are seeking to buy nuclear technology.

As well as the twenty-two arrests, it is believed that the multinational two-year surveillance operation has also led to the recapture of stolen documents, nuclear material and the seizure of eighty million euros in bank accounts belonging to members of the Dark Sun network.

In Britain, police have sealed off Kurt Lydon's Milton Keynes home and uncovered a 'state of the art' computer-aided design facility from which Lydon is believed to have made designs for the Dark Sun network.

Lydon's wife, a surgeon at a Milton Keynes hospital, and his two teenaged children are staying with relatives. When contacted, Dr Lydon refused to make any comment on the search or the arrests.

CHERUB: A HISTORY (1940-1996)

1940   Charles Henderson, a British agent working in Nazi-occupied France, sent a report to his headquarters in London detailing how he'd used children to wangle information out of German soldiers. Upon his return to Britain, Henderson was given permission to form a small undercover detachment of children, under the command of British Military Intelligence. Henderson's Boys were given basic espionage training before being parachuted into occupied France. They gathered vital intelligence in the run-up to the D-Day invasions of 1944.

1946   Henderson's Boys disbanded at the end of the war. Most of them returned to France. Their existence has never been officially acknowledged.

Charles Henderson believed that children would make effective intelligence agents during peacetime. In May 1946, he was given permission to create CHERUB in a disused village school. The first twenty CHERUB recruits, all boys, lived in wooden huts at the back of the playground.

1951 For its first five years, CHERUB struggled along with limited resources. Its fortunes changed following its first major success: two agents uncovered a ring of Russian spies who were stealing information on the British nuclear weapons programme.

The government of the day was delighted. CHERUB was given funding to expand. Better facilities were built and the number of agents was increased from twenty to sixty.

1954 Two CHERUB agents, Jason Lennox and Johan Urminski, were killed while operating undercover in East Germany. Nobody knows how the boys died. The government considered shutting CHERUB down, but there were now over seventy active CHERUB agents performing vital missions around the world.

An inquiry into the boys' deaths led to the introduction of new safeguards:

(1) The creation of the ethics panel. From

now on, every mission had to be approved by a three-person committee.

(2) Jason Lennox was only nine years old. A minimum mission age of ten years and four months was introduced.

(3) A more rigorous approach to training was brought in. A version of the 100-day basic training programme began.

1956 Although many believed that girls would be unsuitable for intelligence work, CHERUB admitted five girls as an experiment. They were a huge success. The number of girls in CHERUB was upped to twenty the following year. Within ten years, the number of girls and boys was equal.

1957 CHERUB introduced its system of coloured T-shirts.

1960 Following several successes, CHERUB was allowed to expand again, this time to 130 students. The farmland surrounding headquarters was purchased and fenced off, about a third of the area that is now known as CHERUB Campus.

1967 Katherine Field became the third CHERUB agent to die on an operation. She was bitten by a snake on a mission in India. She reached hospital within half an hour, but tragically the snake species was wrongly identified and

Katherine was given the wrong anti-venom.

1973 Over the years, CHERUB had become a hotchpotch of small buildings. Construction began on a new nine-storey headquarters.

1977 All cherubs are either orphans, or children who have been abandoned by their family. Max Weaver was one of the first CHERUB agents. He made a fortune building office blocks in London and New York. When he died in 1977, aged just forty-one, without a wife or children, Max Weaver left his fortune for the benefit of the children at CHERUB.

The Max Weaver Trust Fund has paid for many of the buildings on CHERUB campus. These include the indoor athletics facilities and library. The trust fund now holds assets worth over £1 billion.

1982 Thomas Webb was killed by a landmine on the Falkland Islands, becoming the fourth CHERUB agent to die on a mission. He was one of nine agents used in various roles during the Falklands conflict.

1986 The government gave CHERUB permission to expand up to four hundred pupils. Despite this, numbers have stalled some way below this. CHERUB requires intelligent, physically robust agents, who have no family ties. Children who meet all these admission criteria are extremely hard to find.

1990   CHERUB purchased additional land, expanding both the size and security of campus. Campus is marked on all British maps as an army firing range. Surrounding roads are routed so that there is only one road on to campus. The perimeter walls cannot be seen from nearby roads. Helicopters are banned from the area and aeroplanes must stay above ten thousand metres. Anyone breaching the CHERUB perimeter faces life imprisonment under the State Secrets Act.

1996   CHERUB celebrated its fiftieth anniversary with the opening of a diving pool and indoor shooting range.

Every retired member of CHERUB was invited to the celebration. No guests were allowed. Over nine hundred people made it, flying from all over the world. Among the retired agents were a former Prime Minister and a rock guitarist who had sold 80 million albums.

After a firework display, the guests pitched tents and slept on campus. Before leaving the following morning, everyone gathered outside the chapel and remembered the four children who had given CHERUB their lives.

CHERUB: The Recruit

So you've read CHERUB: *Dark Sun*. But how did James Adams end up at CHERUB in the first place?

CHERUB: The Recruit tells James' story from the day his mother dies. Read about his transformation from a couch potato into a skilled CHERUB agent.

Meet Lauren, Jake, Kerry and the rest of the cherubs for the first time, and learn how James foiled the biggest terrorist massacre in British history.

CHERUB: The Recruit available now from Robert Muchamore and Hodder Children's Books.

CHERUB: Class A

Keith Moore is Europe's biggest cocaine dealer. The police have been trying to get enough evidence to nail him for more than twenty years.

Now, four CHERUB agents are joining the hunt. Can a group of kids successfully infiltrate Keith Moore's organisation, when dozens of attempts by undercover police officers have failed?

James Adams has to start at the bottom, making deliveries for small-time drug dealers and getting to know the dangerous underworld they inhabit. He needs to make a big splash if he's going to win the confidence of the man at the top.

CHERUB: Maximum Security

Over the years, CHERUB has put plenty of criminals behind bars. Now, for the first time ever, they've got to break one out . . .

Under American law, kids convicted of serious crimes can be tried and sentenced as adults. Two hundred and eighty of these child criminals live in the sunbaked desert prison known as Arizona Max.

In one of the most daring CHERUB missions ever, James Adams has to go undercover inside Arizona Max, befriend an inmate and then bust him out.

CHERUB: The Killing

When a small-time crook suddenly has big money on his hands, it's only natural that the police want to know where it came from.

James' latest CHERUB mission looks routine: make friends with the bad guy's children, infiltrate his home and dig up some leads for the cops to investigate.

But the plot James begins to unravel isn't what anyone expected. And it seems like the only person who might know the truth is a reclusive eighteen-year-old boy.

There's just one problem. The boy fell from a rooftop and died more than a year earlier.

CHERUB

CHERUB: Divine Madness

When a team of CHERUB agents uncover a link between eco-terrorist group Help Earth and a wealthy religious cult known as The Survivors, James Adams is sent to Australia on an infiltration mission.

It's his toughest job so far. The Survivors' outback headquarters are completely isolated. It's a thousand kilometres to the nearest town and the cult's brainwashing techniques mean James is under massive pressure to conform.

This time he's not just fighting terrorists. He's got to battle to keep control of his own mind.

CHERUB: Man vs Beast

Every day thousands of animals die in laboratory experiments. Some say these experiments provide essential scientific knowledge, while others will do anything to prevent them.

CHERUB agents James and Lauren Adams are stuck in the middle.

CHERUB: The Fall

When an MI5 operation goes disastrously wrong, James needs all of his skills to get out of Russia alive.

Meanwhile, Lauren is on her first solo mission, trying to uncover a brutal human trafficking operation.

And when James does get home, he finds that his nightmare is just beginning . . .

CHERUB: Mad Dogs

The British underworld is controlled by gangs. When two of them start a turf war, violence explodes on to the streets.

The police need information fast and James Adams is the only person who can get it. Returning to the scene of an earlier mission, he has to team up with old friends and face an ex-girlfriend he thought he'd never see again . . .

CHERUB: The Sleepwalker

An airliner explodes over the Atlantic leaving 345 people dead. Crash investigators suspect terrorism, but they're getting nowhere.

A distressed twelve-year-old calls a police hotline and blames his father for the explosion. It could be a breakthrough, but there's no hard evidence and the boy has a history of violence and emotional problems.

Lauren Adams and Jake Parker are sent to investigate, but they hate each other's guts. Meanwhile, James is getting into trouble back on campus . . .

CHERUB: The General

The world's largest urban warfare training compound stands in the desert near Las Vegas. Forty British commandos are being hunted by an entire American battallion.

But their commander has an ace up his sleeve: he plans to smuggle in ten CHERUB agents, and fight the best war game ever.

Look out for *CHERUB: The General*, coming soon from Robert Muchamore and Hodder Children's Books

Think you have what it takes to be a CHERUB agent?

Find out how good you really are, when the biggest mission yet launches in 2008.

For your chance to be part of the action, sign up at
www.cherubmission2008.com

JOIN CHERUB TODAY AT

www.cherubcampus.com

CHERUB campus is the essential internet
destination for all CHERUB fans.
It's packed with exclusive content:
in-depth biographies of CHERUB characters,
out-takes and bonus stories, preview chapters
and all the latest news.

OR TEXT AGENT TO 60022 NOW
UK MOBILES ONLY

This book has been specially written and published for World Book Day 2008.

World Book Day is a worldwide celebration of books and reading. This year is the eleventh anniversary of World Book Day in the United Kingdom and Ireland.

For further information please see
www.worldbookday.com.

World Book Day is made possible by generous sponsorship from National Book Tokens, participating publishers, authors and booksellers. Booksellers who accept the £1 Book Token kindly agree to bear the full cost of redeeming it.